HISTORY SPEAKS
PICTURE BOOKS PLUS READER'S THEATER

Benjamin Brown
AND THE GREAT
STEAMBOAT RACE

BY **SHIRLEY JORDAN**

ILLUSTRATED BY **KATHLEEN KEMLY**

M MILLBROOK PRESS / MINNEAPOLIS

To young readers who want to learn about our proud nation. I hope you will have a chance to see its many wonders. —SJ

For Kim, Dan, Elizabeth, and Sarah —KK

Text copyright © 2011 by Shirley Jordan
Illustrations © 2011 by Lerner Publishing Group, Inc.

Millbrook Press
A division of Lerner Publishing Group, Inc.
241 First Avenue North
Minneapolis, MN 55401 U.S.A.

Website address: www.lernerbooks.com

The author would like to thank Yvonne Knight, administrator of the Howard Steamboat Museum in Jeffersonville, Indiana, for her help with the research for this story.

The image in this book is used with the permission of: © Mary Evans/Pharcide/ The Image Works, p. 33.

Library of Congress Cataloging-in-Publication Data

Jordan, Shirley.
    Benjamin Brown and the great steamboat race / by Shirley Jordan ; illustrated by Kathleen Kemly.
       p. cm. — (History speaks: picture books plus reader's theater)
    Includes bibliographical references.
    ISBN 978–1–58013–674–7 (lib. bdg. : alk. paper)
    1. Natchez (Steamboat)—Juvenile literature. 2. Robert E. Lee (Steamboat)—Juvenile literature. 3. Steamboats—Mississippi River—History—19th century—Juvenile literature. I. Kemly, Kathleen. II. Title.
VM625.M5J67 2011
797.12'5—dc22   2009050055

Manufactured in the United States of America
1 – CG – 12/31/10

CONTENTS

NEW ORLEANS, LOUISIANA

Thursday Afternoon, June 30, 1870

Benjamin pushed through the crowd. If only his mother and father would walk faster!

"I see them! I see them!" Benjamin cried. "There are the red smokestacks. I've found our boat—the *Natchez*."

He squeezed forward for a better look. He was hoping to see the *Natchez's* famous captain, Thomas Leathers. What a fine present for his twelfth birthday! His parents had saved for months to buy three tickets on the *Natchez* for Ben's special day. They were going to travel on the Mississippi River all the way to Saint Louis, Missouri. Saint Louis was 1,270 miles away. If all went well on the river, the trip would take three nights.

Benjamin's father came up behind him. "Well, Ben," he said, "This trip is going to be even more exciting than we thought. We're going to race Captain Cannon's steamboat the *Robert E. Lee*. Men all around us are betting on who will win."

Ben was puzzled. "But Captain Leathers has the gilded antlers. That means he's the captain of the fastest boat on the Mississippi. Why does Captain Cannon want to race us?"

"Well, he must think his boat is faster," his father replied. "If he does win, then Captain Leathers will have to give up his trophy."

Benjamin peered down the row of steamboats. "Which one is the *Robert E. Lee*? I have to see it!"

"They say it's the second boat upriver from here," said his father. "Be careful. Don't get lost in this crowd. I'll take Ma on board the *Natchez* now. You'll find us in Room 7."

Benjamin hurried toward the *Robert E. Lee*. Then he stopped and stared. This steamboat looked as big as the *Natchez*. Like the *Natchez*, it had two side paddle wheels, each as high as the tallest building in New Orleans. But something was wrong.

The *Robert E. Lee* had been stripped of its
doors, windows, and shutters. No cargo sat
waiting to be loaded. Not a passenger was in
sight. Even the anchor was missing. Just one
rope secured the *Robert E. Lee* to the landing.
    "What a strange steamboat," Benjamin thought.
"And what a strange race this will be."

When he returned to the *Natchez*, Benjamin found his
parents in their small cabin. Twenty rooms like theirs faced
a grand salon two hundred feet long. The polished tables
would soon be set for the evening meal. Ma said sometimes
passengers could choose from thirty desserts!

A band began to play "Dixie." Benjamin had heard that
song about a million times. But he couldn't resist tapping his
foot. The two racing steamboats were to leave at five o'clock.
Benjamin and his parents went on deck. The crowd watching
from the riverbank had grown to thousands. Excited voices
rose on the summer air.

"I guess this race up north to Saint Louis is really important," Benjamin thought. "I'm lucky to be going along."

Benjamin caught sight of Captain Leathers high up on the boat's bridge. He was a big man, just as everyone said.

Something large and gold-colored caught Benjamin's attention. The gilded antlers gleamed from the pilothouse.

A loud boom made
Benjamin and his parents
jump. Someone had fired the
deck cannon. The captain
signaled his men to loosen the
mooring ropes, which fastened the
boat to the dock. At exactly five
o'clock, a whistle blew. The *Natchez*
backed away from the dock.

Benjamin turned to his mother. "Listen, Ma," he said. "What they say is true. The whistle sounds just like a huge bumblebee."

Just then, a sailor ran up to the bridge of the *Natchez* and raced toward Captain Leathers. "Captain, sir," the man shouted. "To save time, the *Robert E. Lee*'s mate cut their one rope with an ax. They've left New Orleans four minutes early!"

As the mighty *Natchez* backed away from the landing, it paused. The steamboat shuddered. Then the huge paddle wheels began to creak and turn forward. Benjamin felt both relieved and angry. They just had to catch up with the *Robert E. Lee!* "Captain Cannon isn't playing fair!" Benjamin thought. They moved north. Cheering crowds lined both sides of the river. After his parents left, Benjamin stayed on deck. He was still there as the sky grew dark. Bonfires glowed along the shore where people waited to see the boats.

Benjamin's father suddenly appeared beside him. He had just been in the gentlemen's meeting room. "Bad news, son," Pa said. "Captain Cannon took only a few dozen passengers on his *Robert E. Lee*. He won't stop until Saint Louis. But Captain Leathers plans to make all the regular stops. We have passengers to drop off at each town along the way."

A new wave of anger rushed through Benjamin. It seemed to him that Captain Cannon was cheating.

On Friday, Benjamin and his parents were on deck as the *Natchez* neared Baton Rouge, Louisiana's capital. A small boat passed, heading in the other direction. Benjamin saw a man on board that boat call to the deckhands on the *Natchez*. Then one of the deckhands shouted, "Quick! Tell Captain Leathers! The *Lee* is slowing down. It burst a steam pipe!"

The men on the *Natchez* cheered. They slapped one another on the shoulders. Benjamin whooped with joy. "They'll fix it fast," said his father. "But maybe we can catch them."

From above came the booming voice of Captain Leathers. "Throw on those pine logs, all of them, right in on top of the hot coals. Add some pork fat and that spoiled bacon from the galley."

Black smoke and sparks as big as biscuits poured from the red smokestacks of the *Natchez*. Benjamin held his breath. Sometimes steamboats burst into flames. His father didn't look worried. But Ma sighed and squeezed Ben's hand as they watched the belching smokestacks.

On Saturday, they had almost reached the city of Natchez, Mississippi, when they got more news. Natchez was where steamboats usually stopped for fuel. The *Robert E. Lee* had passed right by the city. Two coal barges had been waiting in the middle of the river for the *Lee*. When it arrived, men tied the barges to the steamboat. They were shoveling coal onto the *Lee* as the mighty steamboat plowed northward. "Oh, no," Benjamin said to his parents when he heard the news. "We have passengers to let off at Natchez and coal to load too!"

Benjamin stood on deck as they pulled up to the dock in Natchez. Captain Leathers had lived here for many years. He'd even named six of his steamboats after the town. His old neighbors wanted Leathers to win. They helped passengers ashore. Men and women grunted as they loaded coal onto the boat in record time.

Even with all of their delays, Ben learned, the *Natchez* was only ten minutes behind! Back on the river, the *Natchez* churned northward. It shook and trembled as its furnaces and boilers worked at full power.

Toward evening, a cold-water pump, which brought water to the boilers, stopped working. "What a time for it to break down!" Benjamin thought. So did everyone else on the *Natchez*. The crew went to work. In thirty minutes, the *Natchez* was back in the race. A smiling Ben hurried back on deck.

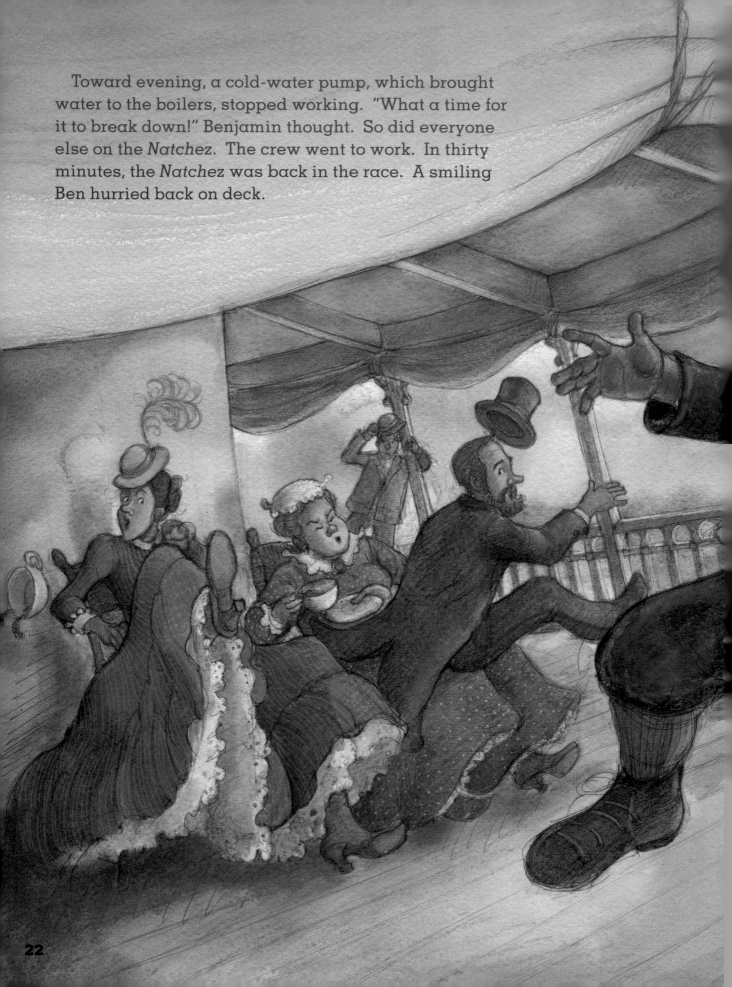

Suddenly, there was a jolt. Ben tumbled backward. Men grabbed for the rail. Ladies screamed. The *Natchez* ground to a halt on top of a sandbar. This ridge of sand just would not let the boat go. How could that happen just as they were catching up!

Benjamin followed the deckhands rushing to the bow of the *Natchez*. He wondered what he could do to help. Captain Leathers ordered the paddle wheels reversed so the boat could back away. But the huge steamboat was stuck fast. They were losing precious time!

Then Benjamin had an idea. What if they could raise the bow of the steamboat while the boat was trying to go backward?

He ran to find his parents. "Ma," he said, "go find your friends in the ladies' drawing room and bring them on deck." He found his father watching a men's card game. "Pa," he panted, "ask the gentlemen to come outside. They can help Captain Leathers. We need everybody!"

In a few minutes, the rear deck filled with passengers. Ben turned to the crowd. "Captain Leathers needs our help," he cried. "If we all stand at the very back of the boat, maybe our weight will make the bow rise."

Men and women began to smile and talk among themselves. They inched closer to the stern. Some called to friends to join them. As the paddle wheels strained in reverse, the steamboat began to inch backward. Slowly, slowly. At last, it was free! Turning with a shudder, the *Natchez* started upstream toward Saint Louis. A cheer went up.

Captain Leathers strode toward Benjamin. "Is this the lad with the good ideas?" he shouted so that everyone would hear. "You'll make a fine steamboat man someday, my boy!"

On Sunday, the day went smoothly. There were no accidents. No bad news about the *Robert E. Lee* came from upriver. But in the evening, a thick fog rolled in.

Such fogs often happened on the Mississippi, and wise captains tied up. There was too much danger under the water. An old tree trunk could tear out the bottom of a steamboat, and passengers might drown.

Ben saw Captain Leathers talking to the crew. The shoulders of the men sagged. It was too dangerous to keep going. They were about 120 miles from Saint Louis.

The crew was tying the boat to a stout tree when Benjamin's father found him. "We might as well get a good sleep, son," he said. "The news is that the *Lee* is still racing up the river in the dark and fog."

On Monday evening, the Fourth of July, Benjamin stood at the rail. He could finally see the lights of Saint Louis. But he wasn't excited. The *Robert E. Lee* had arrived more than six hours earlier. They had lost the race. And Captain Leathers had lost his right to the prized gilded antlers.

Still, it had been a wonderful birthday trip. He loved the smell of the river and the gentle rocking of the steamboat. A tall man joined him at the rail. It was Captain Leathers himself.

"I want to thank you again for helping us off the sandbar," the captain said. "In a few years, when you're ready to try your hand at steamboating, come see me."

"I surely will, sir," Benjamin said, "but I'm sure sorry you lost the antlers."

"Winning isn't everything, son," said the captain. "You have to be proud of the race you ran."

Benjamin knew one thing for sure. Someday, when he became a steamboat captain, he would be an honorable one like Captain Thomas Leathers.

Author's Note

The Great Steamboat Race of 1870 between the *Natchez* and the *Robert E. Lee* was a real event. Benjamin Brown, however, is a fictional character. But he is much like any twelve-year-old boy of that era.

At the time of this story, nearly sixty years had passed since the first steamboat made its journey on the Mississippi. Over the years, these boats grew in size and beauty until they looked like giant floating birthday cakes.

As the boats got bigger, so did the furnaces, which produced heat. This heat raised the water temperature in a steamboat's huge boiler, which made steam. The steam pushed the boat's paddle wheels.

A steamboat could travel at about fifteen miles per hour. When captains raced, they took dangerous chances, adding huge amounts of coal, logs, candles, and even pork fat and other kitchen scraps to make the furnace hotter. Over the years, thousands of passengers died when overloaded furnaces set the wooden steamboats on fire.

But by 1870, passenger travel on the rivers leading to New Orleans had nearly ended, and so had the age of steamboating. Americans were moving west, some to settle new farmland and others to search for gold. There was almost no need for transportation going up and down the Mississippi River.

THE *NATCHEZ (LEFT)* RACES THE *ROBERT E. LEE* IN 1870

To help people traveling westward, thousands of miles of railroad track were laid. In 1855, the first railroad bridge across the Mississippi was completed. More bridges soon followed. The age of steamboating gave way to the age of railroads.

Only a few large paddle wheelers still operate on the Mississippi River. Their cruises last just one or two days. Other steamboats, now restored, have been tied up at river towns and serve as museums or restaurants. A visit to one of these vessels might give you a small taste of the excitement felt by young Benjamin Brown.

Performing Reader's Theater

Dear Student,

Reader's Theater is a dramatic reading. It is a little like a play, but you don't need to memorize your lines. Here are some tips that will help you do your best in a Reader's Theater performance.

BEFORE THE PERFORMANCE

- **Choose your part:** Your teacher may assign parts, or you may be allowed to choose your own part. The character you play does not need to be the same age as you. A boy can play the part of a girl, and a girl can play the part of a boy. That's why it's called acting!

- **Find your lines:** Your character's name is always the same color. The name at the bottom of each page tells you which character has the first line on the next page. If you are allowed to write on your script, highlight your lines. If you cannot write on the script, you may want to use sticky flags to mark your lines.

- **Check pronunciations of words:** If your character's lines include any words you aren't sure how to pronounce, check the pronunciation guide on page 45. If a word isn't there or you still aren't sure how to say it, check a dictionary or ask a teacher, librarian, or other adult.

- **Use your emotions:** Think about how your character feels in the story. If you imagine how your character feels, the audience will hear the emotion in your voice.

- **Use your imagination:** Think about how your character's voice might sound. For example, an old man's voice will sound different from a baby's voice. If you do change your voice, make sure the audience can still understand the words you are saying.

- **Practice your lines:** Even though you do not need to memorize your lines, you should still be comfortable reading them. Read your lines aloud often so they flow smoothly.

DURING THE PERFORMANCE

- **Keep your script away from your face but high enough to read:** If you cover your face with your script, you block your voice from the audience. If you have your script too low, you need to tip your head down farther to read it and the audience won't be able to hear you.

- **Use eye contact:** Good Reader's Theater performers look at the audience as much as they look at their scripts. If you look down, the sound of your voice goes down to the script and not out to the audience.

- **Speak clearly:** Make sure you are loud enough. Say all your words carefully. Be sure not to read too quickly. Remember, if you feel nervous, you may start to speak faster than usual.

- **Use facial expressions and gestures:** Your facial expressions and gestures (hand movements) help the audience know how your character is feeling. If your character is happy, smile. If your character is angry, cross your arms and be sure not to smile.

- **Have fun:** It's okay if you feel nervous. If you make a mistake, just try to relax and keep going. Reader's Theater is meant to be fun for the actors and the audience!

Cast of Characters

NARRATOR 1

NARRATOR 2

NARRATOR 3

BENJAMIN BROWN

MR. BROWN

CAPTAIN LEATHERS

READER:
deckhand, sailor

ALL:
everyone except sound

SOUND:
This part has no lines. The person in this role
is in charge of the sound effects.
Find the sound effects for this script
at www.lerneresource.com.

NARRATOR 1: Benjamin Brown pushed through the crowd along the docks in New Orleans, Louisiana. His mother and father followed behind him.

BEN: I see them! I see them! There are the red smokestacks. I've found our boat, the *Natchez*.

NARRATOR 2: Ben was hoping to see the famous captain of the *Natchez*, Thomas Leathers. What a fine present for his twelfth birthday! His parents had saved for months to buy three tickets on the steamboat.

NARRATOR 3: Ben and his parents lived in New Orleans. They were going to travel on the Mississippi River all the way to Saint Louis, Missouri. Saint Louis was 1,270 miles away. If all went well on the river, the trip would take three nights. Benjamin's father came up behind him.

MR. BROWN: Well, Ben, this trip is going to be even more exciting than we thought. We're going to race Captain Cannon's steamboat the *Robert E. Lee*. Men all around us are betting on who will win.

BEN: But Captain Leathers has the gilded antlers. That means he's the captain of the fastest boat on the Mississippi. Why does Captain Cannon want to race us?

MR. BROWN: He must think his boat is faster. If Cannon wins, then Captain Leathers will have to give up his trophy.

Next Page — **BEN**

BEN: Which one of those steamboats is the *Robert E. Lee*? I have to see it!

MR. BROWN: It's the second boat upriver from here. Be careful. Don't get lost. I'll take Ma on board the *Natchez* now. You'll find us in Room 7.

NARRATOR 1: Benjamin hurried toward the *Robert E. Lee*. The steamboat looked as big as the *Natchez*, and like the *Natchez*, it had two side paddle wheels. Each stood as high as the tallest building in New Orleans. But something was wrong.

NARRATOR 2: The *Robert E. Lee* had been stripped of its doors, windows, and shutters. No cargo sat waiting to be loaded. Not a passenger was in sight. And just one rope secured the *Robert E. Lee* to the landing.

BEN: What a strange steamboat. And what a strange race this will be.

NARRATOR 3: The two racing steamboats were to leave at five o'clock. Benjamin and his parents boarded the *Natchez*. The crowd watching from the riverbank had grown to thousands. Excited voices rose on the summer air.

SOUND: [excited voices]

BEN: I guess this race is really important. I'm lucky to be going along.

NARRATOR 1: Benjamin saw Captain Leathers high up on the boat's bridge. He was a big man, just as everyone said. The gilded antlers gleamed from the pilothouse.

Next Page — **SOUND**

SOUND: [cannon boom]

NARRATOR 2: Benjamin and his parents jumped. Someone had fired the deck cannon. The captain signaled his men to loosen the mooring ropes, which fastened the boat to the dock. At five o'clock, a whistle blew and the *Natchez* backed away from the dock.

SOUND: [whistle]

BEN: What they say is true. The whistle sounds just like a huge bumblebee.

NARRATOR 3: Just then, a sailor raced toward Captain Leathers.

READER (as sailor): Captain, sir. To save time, the *Robert E. Lee*'s mate cut their one rope with an ax. They've left New Orleans four minutes early!

NARRATOR 1: The mighty *Natchez* shuddered as it backed away from the landing. Then the huge paddle wheels began to creak and turn forward. Benjamin felt relieved but angry.

BEN: Captain Cannon isn't playing fair! We just have to catch up with the *Robert E. Lee*!

NARRATOR 2: The boat moved north, and Benjamin stayed on deck as the sky grew dark. Benjamin's father suddenly appeared beside him. He had just been in the gentlemen's meeting room.

Next Page — **MR. BROWN**

MR. BROWN: Bad news, son. Captain Cannon took only a few dozen passengers on his *Robert E. Lee.* He won't stop until Saint Louis. But Captain Leathers plans to make all the regular stops. We have passengers to drop off at each town along the way.

BEN: Captain Cannon is cheating!

NARRATOR 3: The next day, the *Natchez* neared Baton Rouge, Louisiana's capital. A small boat passed, heading in the other direction. A man on board that boat called to the deckhands on the *Natchez.* One of the deckhands shouted out to the people on deck.

READER (as deckhand): Tell Captain Leathers! The *Lee* is slowing down. It burst a steam pipe!

SOUND: [crowd cheers]

NARRATOR 1: The men on the *Natchez* slapped one another on the shoulders. Benjamin whooped with joy.

BEN: Hooray!

MR. BROWN: They'll fix it fast. But maybe we can catch them.

NARRATOR 2: Then from above came the booming voice of Captain Leathers.

CAPTAIN LEATHERS: Grab those pine logs. Throw them right on top of the hot coals.

Next Page — **NARRATOR 3**

NARRATOR 3: Black smoke poured from the smokestacks of the *Natchez*. Benjamin held his breath. Sometimes steamboats burst into flames. His father didn't look worried. But his mother sighed and squeezed Ben's hand.

NARRATOR 1: By the next morning, they had almost reached the city of Natchez, Mississippi. Natchez was where steamboats usually stopped for fuel. Suddenly a deckhand gave Ben more news.

READER (as deckhand): The *Robert E. Lee* had passed right by Natchez. Two coal ships had been waiting in the middle of the river for the *Lee*. When it arrived, men tied the ships to the steamboat. They shoveled coal onto the *Lee* as it moved northward.

BEN: Oh, no. We have passengers to let off at Natchez and coal to load too!

NARRATOR 2: Benjamin stood on deck as they pulled up to the dock in Natchez. Captain Leathers had lived here for many years. He'd even named six of his steamboats after the town. Leathers's old neighbors wanted Leathers to win.

NARRATOR 3: They helped passengers ashore. Volunteers grunted as they loaded coal onto the boat in record time.

READER (as deckhand): Even with all the delays, we're only ten minutes behind!

NARRATOR 1: Back on the river, the *Natchez* churned northward. It shook and trembled as its furnaces and boilers worked at full power. Toward evening, a cold-water pump, which brought water to the boilers, stopped working.

Next Page — **BEN**

BEN: What a time for it to break down!

NARRATOR 2: The crew went to work. In thirty minutes, the *Natchez* was back in the race. A smiling Ben hurried back on deck. Suddenly, there was a jolt.

SOUND: [jolt]

NARRATOR 3: Ben tumbled backward. Men grabbed for the rail. Ladies screamed. The *Natchez* ground to a halt on top of a sandbar. This ridge of sand would not let the boat go.

BEN: Just as we were catching up!

NARRATOR 1: Benjamin followed the deckhands rushing to the bow of the *Natchez*.

BEN: I wonder how I can help.

LEATHERS: Sailors, listen up! Reverse the paddle wheels. Then the boat can back away.

READER (as sailor): We can't, the boat is stuck. We're losing time!

NARRATOR 2: Suddenly Ben had an idea. He ran to find his parents.

BEN: What if we raise the bow of the steamboat while the boat is trying to go backward? Ma, go find your friends in the ladies' drawing room and bring them on deck. Pa, ask the gentlemen to come outside. They can all help!

NARRATOR 3: In a few minutes, the rear deck filled with passengers. Ben turned to the crowd.

Next Page — **BEN**

BEN: Captain Leathers needs our help. If we all stand at the very back of the boat, maybe our weight will make the bow rise.

SOUND: [crowd murmur]

NARRATOR 1: Men and women inched closer to the boat's stern. Some called to friends to join them. As the paddle wheels strained in reverse, the steamboat began to slowly inch backward. At last, it was free!

NARRATOR 2: The *Natchez* turned with a shudder. Then it started upstream toward Saint Louis. A cheer went up. Captain Leathers strode toward Benjamin.

LEATHERS: Is this the lad with the good ideas? You'll make a fine steamboat man someday!

NARRATOR 3: There were no accidents the next day. No bad news about the *Robert F. Lee* came from upriver. But in the evening, a thick fog rolled in. Fogs often happened on the Mississippi, and wise captains tied up. There was too much danger under the water.

NARRATOR 1: An old tree trunk hidden in the water could tear out the bottom of a steamboat. Passengers might drown. Ben saw Captain Leathers talking to the crew. The shoulders of the men sagged. It was too dangerous to keep going. They were about 120 miles from Saint Louis. The crew was tying the boat to a tree when Benjamin's father found him.

Next Page — **MR. BROWN**

MR. BROWN: We might as well get a good sleep, son. The news is that the *Lee* is still racing up the river in the dark and fog.

NARRATOR 2: On Monday evening, the Fourth of July, Benjamin stood at the rail. He could finally see the lights of Saint Louis. But he wasn't excited. The *Robert E. Lee* had arrived more than six hours earlier.

NARRATOR 3: They had lost the race. And Captain Leathers had lost his right to the prized gilded antlers. But it had been a wonderful birthday trip. Ben loved the smell of the river and the gentle rocking of the steamboat. A tall man joined him at the rail. It was Captain Leathers himself.

LEATHERS: Thank you again for helping us off the sandbar. When you're ready to try your hand at steamboating, come see me.

BEN: I surely will, sir. But I'm sure sorry you lost the antlers.

LEATHERS: Winning isn't everything, son. You have to be proud of the race you ran.

NARRATOR 1: Benjamin knew one thing for sure. Someday, when he became a steamboat captain, he would be an honorable one like Captain Thomas Leathers.

ALL: The end

Pronunciation Guide

Baton Rouge: BA-tuhn ROOZH
bow: BOW (rhymes with cow)

Natchez: NA-chehz
Saint Louis: SAYNT LOO-ihs
whooped: WOOPT

Glossary

boiler: a tank in which water is boiled to produce steam power

bow: the front part of a boat or a ship

bridge: a raised area near the front of a boat that contains the pilothouse

cargo: the load of goods carried by a boat or a ship

deckhands: sailors who do most of their work on the main deck of a boat

furnace: a metal chamber in which fuel is burned to produce heat

galley: the kitchen of a ship or a boat

gilded: covered with a thin layer of gold or gold-colored paint

on board: located on a boat or a ship

paddle wheels: wheels with flat boards attached that push against the water and make a steamboat move

pilothouse: the place on a boat where the steering wheel and the compass are located

riverbank: a stretch of land along the edge of a river

sandbar: a ridge of sand formed in a river by the action of currents

stern: the rear end of a boat or a ship

upriver: against the current of a river

Selected Bibliography

Andrist, Ralph K., *Steamboats on the Mississippi*. New York: American Heritage, 1962.

Donovan, Frank. *River Boats of America*. New York: Thomas Y. Crowell, 1966.

Gandy, Joan W., and Thomas H. Gandy. *The Mississippi Steamboat Era in Historic Photographs*. New York: Dover, 1987.

Havighurst, Walter. *Voices on the River: The Story of the Mississippi Waterways*. New York: Macmillan, 1964.

Keating, Bern. *The Mighty Mississippi*. Washington, DC: National Geographic Society, 1971.

Price, Willard. *The Amazing Mississippi*. New York: John Day Company, 1963.

Further Reading and Websites

BOOKS

Bowen, Andy Russell. *A Head Full of Notions: A Story about Robert Fulton*. Minneapolis: Millbrook Press, 1997. Here you can read the story of the famous young Pennsylvania inventor with a talent for making machines. Robert Fulton designed one of the earliest steamboats.

Esbaum, Jill. *Ste-e-e-e-eamboat a Comin'*. New York: Farrar, Straus & Giroux, 2005. This rhyming picture book is a fictional story about steamboats on the Mississippi.

Hartford, John. *Steamboat in a Cornfield*. New York: Crown, 1986. This book tells the true story in rhyme of a steamboat.

Stein, R. Conrad. *The Story of Mississippi Steamboats*. Chicago: Children's Press, 1987. This book gives a brief history of the steamboats on the Mississippi River from the early to mid 1800s.

St. George, Judith. *The Amazing Voyage of the New Orleans*. New York: G. P. Putnam's Sons, 1980. This story tells of the 1811 voyage of the *New Orleans*, the first steamboat to travel down the Ohio and Mississippi rivers.

Websites

Dave Thomson Collection
http://www.steamboats.com/museum/davet1000.html
This site offers high-resolution photos of four famous steamboats. Each photo shows a lot of detail and can be printed out to fit an 8½-by-11-inch sheet of paper.

The Howard Steamboat Museum, Jefferson, Indiana
http://www.steamboatmuseum.org/
This website offers easy-to-read information and illustrations from a private museum. Click on "Photo Album" and then "Howard Boats" to see a wonderful collection of old steamboat photos.

Steamboating on the Mississippi
http://www.usgennet.org/usa/mo/county/stlouis/steamboat.htm
This website contains historical tidbits about the early steamboat days in Saint Louis. The background music is the lively tune "Steamboat Bill."

Steamboat Learning Center, Floating Classroom
http://steamboats.com/research/index.html
This is a page for students who want to research steamboats. It gives ideas for school reports and offers prompts to help a student begin research and writing.

Dear Teachers and Librarians,

Congratulations on bringing Reader's Theater to your students! Reader's Theater is an excellent way for your students to develop their reading fluency. Phrasing and inflection, two important reading skills, are at the heart of Reader's Theater. Students also develop public speaking skills such as volume, pacing, and facial expression.

The traditional format of Reader's Theater is very simple. There really is no right or wrong way to do it. By following these few tips, you and your students will be ready to explore the world of Reader's Theater.

EQUIPMENT

Location: A theater or gymnasium is a fine place for a Reader's Theater performance, but staging the performance in the classroom works well too.

Scripts: Each reader will need a copy of the script. Scripts that are individually printed should be bound into binders that allow the readers to turn the pages easily. Printable scripts for all the books in this series are available at www.lerneresource.com.

Music Stands: Music stands are very helpful for the readers to set their scripts on.

Costumes: Traditional Reader's Theater does not use costumes. Dressing uniformly, such as all wearing the same color shirt, will give a group a polished look. Specific costume pieces can be used when a reader is performing multiple roles. They help the audience follow the story.

Props: Props are optional. If necessary, readers may mime or gesture to convey objects that are important to the story. Props can be used much like a costume piece to identify different characters performed by one reader. Prop suggestions for each story are available at www.lerneresource.com.

Background and Sound Effects: These aren't essential, but they can add to the fun of Reader's Theater. Customized backgrounds for each story in this series and sound effects corresponding to the scripts are available at www.lerneresource.com. You will need a screen or electronic whiteboard for the background. You will need a computer with speakers to play the sound effects.

PERFORMANCE

Staging: Readers usually face the audience in a straight line or a semicircle. If the readers are using music stands, the stands should be raised chest high. A stand should not block a reader's mouth or face, but it should allow for the reader to read without looking down too much. The main character is usually placed in the center. The narrator is on the end. In the case of multiple narrators, place one narrator on each end.

Reading: Reader's Theater scripts do not need to be memorized. However, the readers should be familiar enough with the script to maintain a fair amount of eye contact with the audience. Encourage readers to act with their voices by reading with inflection and emotion.

Blocking (stage movement): For traditional Reader's Theater, there are no blocking cues to follow. You may want to have the students turn the pages simultaneously. Some groups prefer that readers sit or turn their back to the audience when their characters are "offstage" or have left a scene. Some groups will have their readers move about the stage, script in hand, to interact with the other readers. The choice is up to you.

Overture and Curtain Call: Before the performance, a member of the group should announce the title and the author of the piece. At the end of the performance, all readers step in front of their music stands, stand in a line, grasp hands, and bow in unison.

LERNER

SOURCE

Please visit www.lerneresource.com for printable scripts, prop suggestions, sound effects, a background image that can be projected on a screen or electronic whiteboard, a Reader's Theater teacher's guide, and reading-level information for all roles.

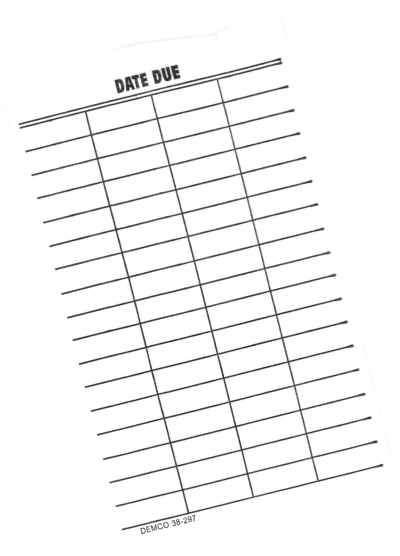

DEMCO 38-297